Clifford's
Valentines

Copyright © 2001 by Norman Bridwell.

All rights reserved. Published by Scholastic Inc.
SCHOLASTIC, CARTWHEEL BOOKS, and associated logos
are trademarks and/or registered trademarks of Scholastic Inc.
CLIFFORD, CLIFFORD THE BIG RED DOG, and associated logos
are trademarks and/or registered trademarks of Norman Bridwell.
Lexile is a registered trademark of MetaMetrics, Inc.

Library of Congress Cataloging-in-Publication Data is available.

ISBN-13: 978-0-439-18300-0
ISBN-10: 0-439-18300-6

28 27 26 25 24 23   12 13 14 15 16/0

Printed in the U.S.A. 40 • This edition first printing, August 2008

NORMAN BRIDWELL
Clifford's
Valentines

Cartwheel B·O·O·K·S ®

SCHOLASTIC INC.

New York   Toronto   London   Auckland   Sydney
Mexico City   New Delhi   Hong Kong   Buenos Aires

It is Valentine's Day.

Clifford gets a card.
It is from a boy.

Clifford gets a card.
It is from a girl.

Clifford gets a card
from a woman.

Clifford gets a card
from a man.

The letter carrier comes.

Now Clifford gets many, many more cards.
Everyone loves Clifford!

It starts to snow.

It snows and snows.
Clifford has an idea.

He runs to the park.

The boy, the girl, the woman, and the man are there.

Many, many other people are there, too.

Clifford makes a heart in the snow.

Happy Valentine's Day, everyone!

• Word List •

a	it
an	letter
and	loves
are	makes
boy	man
card	many
carrier	more
Clifford	now
comes	other
day	park
everyone	people
from	runs
gets	snow
girl	starts
happy	the
has	there
heart	to
idea	too
in	Valentine's
is	woman